STEEL TOWN

ATHENEUM BOOKS FOR YOUNG READERS
An imprint of Simon & Schuster Children's Publishing Division
1230 Avenue of the Americas, New York, New York 10020

Book design by Debra Sfetsios
The text for this book is set in Industrial 736.
The illustrations for this book are rendered in acrylic on paper.
A special thanks to the Art Institute of McKinney.
Manufactured in China
First Edition
2 4 6 8 10 9 7 5 3 1
Library of Congress Cataloging-in-Publication Data
Winter, Jonah.
Steel Town / Jonah Winter ; illustrated by Terry Widener. —1st ed.
p. cm.
Summary: In Steel Town, it's always raining, freight trains come and go, the big furnace roars, and
the steel mill never sleeps.
ISBN-13: 978-1-4169-4081-4
ISBN-10: 1-4169-4081-2
[1. Mills and mill work—Fiction. 2. Cities and towns—Fiction.] I. Widener, Terry, ill. II. Title.
PZ7.W75477Ste 2008
[E]—dc22
2006029284

FOR LITTLE BUDDY BARTRUM—J. W.

To Lynn, Smylee, and Maple—T. W.

STEEL TOWN

BY JONAH WINTER

ILLUSTRATED BY TERRY WIDENER

ATHENEUM BOOKS FOR YOUNG READERS
New York LONDON Toronto SYDNEY

In Steel Town, it's always dark
and the street-lamps are always lit.

At dawn, the workers get out of bed
and take the stairs down Goat Path Hill,
down to their jobs at the iron and steel mills.
Each man carries a Thermos full of coffee,
hot and black, black and hot.

Other men, tired and dirty,
walk up the stairs, coming home
from the late-night shift,
ready for bed, ready for sleep.

Down below, down in the valley,
black smoke puffs from the smokestacks.
In Steel Town, the mills never sleep.

In Steel Town, it's always raining,
but no one carries an umbrella.
You walk beneath the railroad trestle
then walk back into the rain.
Your face stays the same.

In Steel Town, there's the steel mill
and the iron mill.
If you work at the steel mill,
you stay on this side.
If you work at the iron mill,
you make your way across the Birmingham Bridge.

Barges carrying coal
go up and down the Pitch-Black River
all day long, all night long,
carrying coal from
the Midnight Mountains
way up yonder, far away.

In Steel Town,
freight trains carrying coal and steel
are always grinding in and out of the mills,
all day long, all night long,
squeaking and grinding and rumbling by,
squeaking and grinding and rumbling by.

Big heaps of coal
are what you see
as you get near the iron mill:
coal heaps, coal heaps,
and iron ore heaps.

Inside the iron mill,
it's like another world:
fire and smoke,
fire and smoke.
No matter the time of day or night,
the men keep working,
the machines don't stop:
fire and smoke,
fire and smoke.

The coal comes rolling into the mill
on a little train they call the "larry."
The coal goes into the Beehive Oven
and gets turned into a thing called "coke."

One man scrapes the coke out
and onto a rolling conveyor belt.
One man makes the conveyor belt go.
One man gets the boxcar ready
and the coke gets dumped in the boxcar.
Iron ore goes in another boxcar.
Limestone goes in another boxcar.
These are the things you need to make iron.

The Boxcar Man straightens his hat
and puts his train into gear.
The boxcars go to the center of the mill,
to the place where they make the iron:
the mighty, fiery Blast Furnace.

The Skip Hoist Operator operates the skip hoist
that carries the iron ore
and coke and limestone
all the way up to the top.

The Hot Blast Operator
blasts hot air into the Blast Furnace—
until the inside gets hot as blazes,
3,000 degrees.

Outside the furnace, it's so hot,
you have to wear
a big, heavy, fireproof suit
from head to toe.
Inside that suit, it's hotter
than the hottest desert.
Outside the furnace, it's so hot,
you'd die
if you took the suit off.

Outside the furnace, it's so loud,
you can't hear anything
except for the roar.
You can't talk.
You can't do anything
except for work,
work and sweat,
work and sweat.

One man peeps through a little peephole
into the inside part of the furnace.
What he sees is molten iron,
ready to pour,
ready to tap.

He signals to the Monkey Boss,
who drills through a plug in the side of the furnace.
That's called "tapping the furnace."
Hot "pig-iron" comes gushing out.
Pig-iron's what they call it
before it gets turned into steel.
It runs in a flaming river
down through a gutter on the floor.

Men step through the molten iron
wearing big wooden shoes
so their feet don't get burned.
They skim the slag off the top of the iron.
The slag is what they don't want.

Red and writhing, molten pig-iron
snakes its way through a hole in the floor
and down into the ladle cars,
waiting to be filled.

When the ladle cars are full,
the foreman signals to the Hot-Car Man,
and he pulls the lever,
and off goes the train . . .

off goes the train across the Hot Metal Bridge
and over the Pitch-Black River
to the place where the pig-iron gets turned into steel:
the steel mill.

Inside the steel mill,
the Crane Man waits
for the Hot-Car Man.
When the train is in place,
the Crane Man pulls a lever:
The big crane picks up each big ladle
sloshing full of molten pig-iron
and dumps it into the Open Hearth Furnace.

This is how they make the steel.
Inside the hearth, the pig-iron bubbles
along with lots of other stuff
that'll turn that pig-iron into steel.
When the hearth is full,
a man taps the plug

and out comes the steel,
hot as fire, hot as fire,
flowing into another big ladle
that dumps it all
into smaller vats
5 tons each,
about the size of two men.

Just like clockwork, just like clockwork,
the Crane Man hoists the small vats
onto another train.
Just like clockwork, just like clockwork,
the Rail-Tractor Man
hauls the small vats away.

The steam whistle blows.

LUNCH BREAK!

At the Mill Canteen,
you can get a 5-cent hot dog.
You can drink your coffee.
And if there's time,
you can play a game of cards.

When lunch break is over, though,
it's hard work again—
back to the fire,
back to the roar.

This is where it all begins:
big beams used to make buildings
and bridges
and railroad rails,
big sheets used to make cars
and ships
and airplanes
and cans that food goes into.
Steel, steel, everywhere steel.
This is where it all begins.

These are the men who make the steel.
Strong backs, bones, muscles, and sweat
are what make the steel.
One man, two men, three men, four men
move it along
on the rolling mills
till it's lifted by cranes
into railroad cars

and taken away
to the other world
beyond the Midnight Mountains.

And another shift is over.

Time to punch the time-card.
Time to get paid:
Three crinkly bills
in a grimy hand.
That means food.

THAT MEANS TIME TO GO HOME.

In Steel Town,
at the end of the day,
you walk past a church
with an onion-shaped dome
right next-door to the mill.

Inside the open doors,
you see old Russian ladies
praying and whispering,
lighting candles.

A few doors down from the church,
you walk past the neighborhood pool hall.
Maybe you step inside for a game.
Maybe you sit down and rest for a while.

Then comes the slow climb
back up the hillside,
back up the stairs.
And the evening shift
is going down.

On Goat Path Hill, where the workers live,
the skinniest houses in the world
stand side by side,
crowded together.

On Grapevine Lane,
neighbors talk
over backyard fences,
trading things from their gardens:
green peppers, red tomatoes,
onions and figs, buckets of grapes.

In Steel Town,
the men sit down
while the women cook.
In one house,
they cook big pots of red spaghetti sauce.

Next door,
they cook big pots of pierogies,
which are little Polish dumplings
stuffed with potatoes
and covered with butter and onions.

After dinner,
people sit on porches
and watch the rain fall
over the steel mill,
over the iron mill,
down in the valley.

Someone's radio
is always playing
off in the distance:
*"Every time it rains, it rains
pennies from heaven . . ."*

In Steel Town,
the iron and steel mills never sleep.
But sometimes,
the people do.

Good night, Steel Town.

12/08

ML